NO BORING STORIES!

WORDS BY
JULIE FALATKO

PICTURES BY
CHARLES SANTOSO

VIKING

VIKING

Penguin Young Readers

An imprint of Penguin Random House LLC

375 Hudson Street

New York, New York 10014

First published in the United States of America by Viking,

an imprint of Penguin Random House LLC, 2018

Text copyright © 2018 by Julie Falatko

Illustrations copyright © 2018 by Charles Santoso

LIBRARY OF CONGRESS CATALOGING-IN-PUBLICATION DATA IS AVAILABLE

ISBN 9780451476821

Manufactured in China   Set in Josefin Slab   Book design by Jim Hoover

10   9   8   7   6   5   4   3   2   1

For Joanna, who read my book where strange
stuff happens and saw what it could be. —J.F.

For Jen, who accepts me as I am.   —C.S.

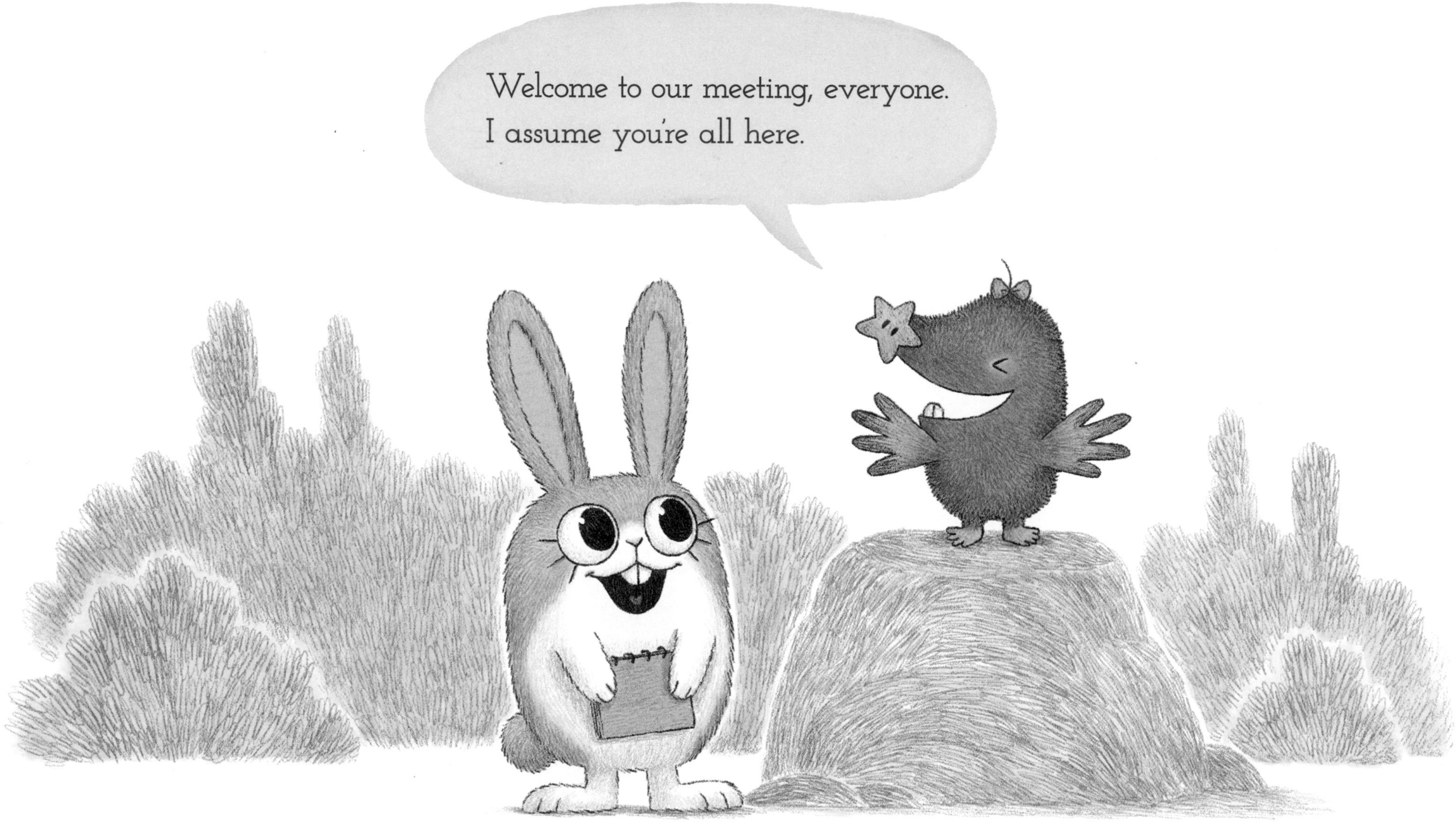
Welcome to our meeting, everyone. I assume you're all here.

Sniff

Sniff,
Sniff

!!!

YOU'RE A BUNNY!
Intruder! Alert!
If you please, Miss Mole, I'd like to–

I can guess why you're here! You want to bore us with your stories of cuddling and mommies and kittens and bedtime! We don't need your help. Please go!

I don't see anyone except for you.

Everyone else will be here in a minute.

I'll start, honey. Princess Babirusa, strong and fierce, must battle to save her kingdom.

And her kingdom's sandwiches!

She assembles her most trusted confidants to fight with her.

The first is a brilliant and handsome giraffe-necked weevil who, as the largest weevil in the world—

Holy crabs, I've never seen one up close!
She's got a notebook! Are you stealing our ideas to make your stories more interesting?
This is where I write my own interesting stories.

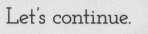

Let's continue.

The next friend to join the fight is an awesome yeti crab who builds a giant robot suit to shoot at the humongous grape monsters who are trying to steal the sandwiches, and there are lasers on the arms and he's all **BAM! WHIZZ! PFOO!**

And then the evil grapes go underground to escape the rain of laser fire, only to meet the last member of the princess's posse, a star-nosed mole who digs faster than lightning and confuses the grapes with her maze of burrows.
And then they fight with carrots! Which grow underground!

What?

My story has carrots and sandwiches too.

And then the rest of it is about friendship and sharing and hugging, I'm sure.

I wonder if we could make carrot weapons that shoot lasers.

I'd read that story!

Relatable characters!

Check! She's feisty, beautiful, and clever.

Inciting incident!

That is clearly when the gigantic grapes viciously attack the innocent kingdom.

...ZZZZZZ

Those are boring stories! I like books where strange stuff happens. But everyone says my stories are too weird.

I think weird stories are cool.

Remember the one you wrote where the main character was a discarded shoe who loved to sing?

That sounds hilarious!

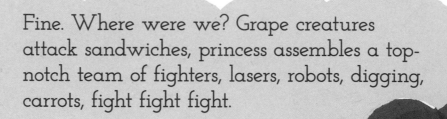

How about this?
The handsome weevil comes in on a shining steed and carries them all to safety.

And the princess declares that the grapes are no good.

Then what?

Then the grapes are humiliated and go back to their planet?

PLANET of THE GRAPES!

None of these ideas are any good.

And so the stealthy bunny poked at the evil grapes with her carrot swords—*HIYA!*—and the grapes retreated to the surface, only to be dried into raisins by the yeti crab's lasers and chopped to bits by the giraffe-necked weevil's mandibles and mixed with mayo and shredded carrot swords by Princess Babirusa.

And they all celebrated with an enormous feast of carrot raisin salad sandwiches.

But if a bunch of adorable frogs and puppies show up next week wanting to work on their stories about birthday parties, you're out.

It's a deal.